For the children and the trees

The Sierra Club, founded in 1892 by John Muir, has devoted itself to the study and protection of the earth's scenic and ecological resources—mountains, wetlands, woodlands, wild shores and rivers, deserts and plains. The publishing program of the Sierra Club offers books to the public as a nonprofit educational service in the hope that they may enlarge the public's understanding of the Club's basic concerns. The Sierra Club has some sixty chapters in the United States and in Canada. For information about how you may participate in its programs to preserve wilderness and the quality of life, please address inquiries to Sierra Club, 730 Polk Street, San Francisco, CA 94109.

First Edition

The Forgotten Forest was edited, designed, and produced by Frances Lincoln Ltd., Apollo Works, 5 Charlton Kings Road, London NW5 2SB.

Library of Congress Cataloging-in-Publication Data

Anholt, Laurence.
        The forgotten forest / Laurence Anholt. — 1st ed.
            p.   cm.
        Summary: The vast forests of a country are all cut down to make room for development, until finally only one small wooded area remains like an island in the endless noisy sea of the city.
        ISBN 0-87156-569-2
        [1. Forests and forestry—Fiction. 2. Forests conservation—Fiction. 3. Conservation of natural resources—Fiction.]
        I. Title.
        PZ7.A58635Fo 1992
        [E]—dc20   91-21293

Printed in Hong Kong

10 9 8 7 6 5 4 3 2 1

For the children and the trees

The Sierra Club, founded in 1892 by John Muir, has devoted itself to the study and protection of the earth's scenic and ecological resources—mountains, wetlands, woodlands, wild shores and rivers, deserts and plains. The publishing program of the Sierra Club offers books to the public as a nonprofit educational service in the hope that they may enlarge the public's understanding of the Club's basic concerns. The Sierra Club has some sixty chapters in the United States and in Canada. For information about how you may participate in its programs to preserve wilderness and the quality of life, please address inquiries to Sierra Club, 730 Polk Street, San Francisco, CA 94109.

First Edition

The Forgotten Forest was edited, designed, and produced by Frances Lincoln Ltd., Apollo Works, 5 Charlton Kings Road, London NW5 2SB.

Library of Congress Cataloging-in-Publication Data

Anholt, Laurence.
    The forgotten forest / Laurence Anholt. — 1st ed.
        p.   cm.
    Summary: The vast forests of a country are all cut down to make room for development, until finally only one small wooded area remains like an island in the endless noisy sea of the city.
        ISBN 0-87156-569-2
        [1. Forests and forestry—Fiction. 2. Forests conservation—Fiction. 3. Conservation of natural resources—Fiction.]
    I. Title.
    PZ7.A58635Fo 1992
    [E]—dc20   91-21293

Printed in Hong Kong

10 9 8 7 6 5 4 3 2 1

THE
Forgotten
Forest

Laurence Anholt

Sierra Club Books for Children
San Francisco

A long time ago, but not so far away, there was a country that was covered by trees.

People used to say that a squirrel could leap from branch to branch, right from one coast to the other.

The great forests were often full of the sounds of
children laughing — and sometimes the chopping of axes

as trees were cleared to make way for houses.
There were so many trees that it didn't seem to matter.

And the trees could not complain — even when whole forests were cleared to make way for towns.

Year in, year out. A leaf for every brick.

Until, one day, there was only a single forest left —

one small forest like an island in the endless, noisy sea
of the city.

And everyone had forgotten it was there. No one had time
to think about trees anymore.

Everyone had forgotten — except the children.

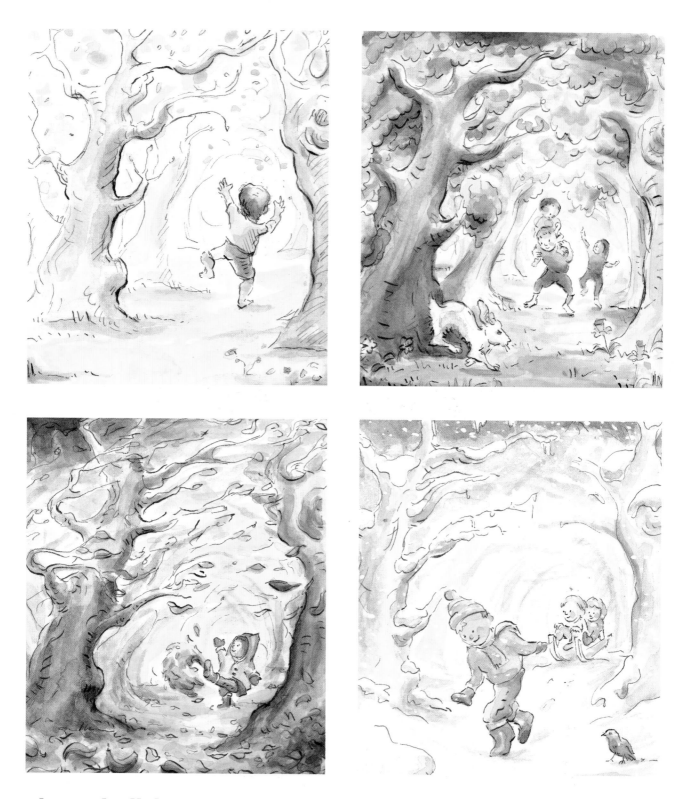

Through all the seasons of the year,

the children played in the forgotten forest.

Then, one day, a terrible thing happened. A man hung a notice on the forest fence. It said: BUILDING STARTS TOMORROW.

If the trees could have talked, they would have cried out then.

The builders opened the gate into the forest . . .
and were amazed by what they found. It was all
so peaceful, so silent.

But listen! There *was* a noise — at first a whispering in the leaves, then a sighing, then a crying. It grew louder and louder, until it sounded as though the whole forest was weeping.

And there, in the very center of the forest, were all the children.
It was the children crying for the trees.

"Come on!" shouted a man. "We have seen enough."
"Yes!" said the other builders. "We must start work right away."

But it was not the trees they pulled down —

it was the fence around them.

The children danced with joy — but the work had only begun. "We will plant new trees!" the builders shouted. "A tree for every child. Trees on every street. Who will help? Will *you* help?"

And in the forgotten forest there was a whispering, then a chuckling. It grew louder and louder, until it sounded as though the whole forest was laughing.
Or was it just the children playing among the trees?